מסורה

ArtScroll Youth Series®

MITZVOS WE CAN DO

By Yaffa Rosenthal

Illustrated by
Rabbi Shmuel Kunda

Published by

Mesorah Publications, ltd

אבגדהוזחטיכלמנסעפצקרשת

For my children —
Yisrael Meir, Hadassah, Esther Leeba, Avrahom Shalom

I wish to take this opportunity to express my deepest feelings of gratitude and love for my wonderful parents, Leon and Rachel Faigenbam, who have always done everything with מסירות נפש for me. I will forever appreciate their love and devotion. May HASHEM bless them now and forever with all that is good.

I could never adequately express my sincere appreciation to my special parents-in-law, Samuel and Miriam Rosenthal. May HASHEM bestow good health, well-being and endless ברכות upon them for their tireless devotion.

To my dedicated teachers in Cleveland, Ohio at Yeshivath Adath B'nai Israel, The Hebrew Academy, and at Yavne — may HASHEM reward you forever for inspiring me to love Torah and mitzvos.

It is my wish that this book bring our children to observe the mitzvos of the Torah and fulfill them out of love for HASHEM. May HASHEM, Who is כלו חסד, delight in their mitzvos and מעשים טובים, and grant us all our most fervent desire — that Mashiach come to redeem us speedily, in our days. אמן

Chaya Yaffa Rosenthal

FIRST EDITION
First Impression ... November 1982
Second Impression ... September 1984
Third Impression ... January 1988
Fourth Impression ... November 2002

Published and Distributed by
MESORAH PUBLICATIONS, LTD.
4401 Second Avenue / Brooklyn, N.Y 11232

Distributed in Europe by
LEHMANNS
Unit E, Viking Industrial Park
Rolling Mill Road NE32 3DP
Jarow, Tyne & Wear, England

Distributed in Israel by
SIFRIATI / A. GITLER BOOKS
6 Hayarkon Street
Bnei Brak 51127

Distributed in Australia and New Zealand by
GOLDS WORLD OF JUDAICA
3-13 William Street
Balaclava, Melbourne 3183
Victoria Australia

Distributed in South Africa by
KOLLEL BOOKSHOP
Shop 8A Norwood Hypermarket
Norwood 2196, Johannesburg, South Africa

Typography by *CompuScribe* at ArtScroll Studios, Ltd.
Printed in the United States of America

What is a mitzvah?

A mitzvah is something
HASHEM wants us to do.

All the mitzvos we have are good for me and you.
There are so many mitzvos!
HASHEM wants us to keep all of them.

Now come with me
and I'll show you from א to ת
some of the mitzvos of HASHEM.

ד	ה	ו
י	כ	ל
ס	ע	פ
ר	שׁ	ת

אבג

זחט

מנ

צק

אֱמֶת
Truth

HASHEM wants you always to tell the truth.
Please don't ever tell a lie.

א ב ג ד ה ו ז ח ט י כ ל מ נ ס ע פ צ ק ר ש ת

בְּרָכוֹת
Blessings

And He is listening to you
when you say a brachah (blessing)
to thank Him for an apple or ice cream or pie.

א **ב** גדהוזחטיכלמנסעפצקרשת

גְּמִילוּת חֲסָדִים
Acts of Kindness

Did you know that you can help other people
in so many ways?

אבגדההוזחטיכלמנסעפצקרשת

דִּיבּוּר יָפֶה

Speaking Nicely

And when you talk,
be sure that good things are all that you say.

אבגדהוזחטיכלמנסעפצקרשת

הַכְנָסַת אוֹרְחִים

ה

Welcoming Guests

When a guest comes over
try to make him feel good, and you'll feel good too.

אבגד**ה**וזחטיכלמנסעפצקרשת

וִידּוּי

Regret for Wrong Deeds

Sometimes we have to tell HASHEM we are sorry
for the wrong things we do.

אבגדהוזחטיכלמנסעפצקרשת

זָכוֹר אֶת יוֹם הַשַּׁבָּת   ז
Remember the Shabbos Day

To remember Shabbos (the Sabbath)
and make it a special day means you are a real Jew!

אבגדהוזחטיכלמנסעפצקרשת

חֲנֻכָּה
Chanukah

Isn't lighting the Chanukah menorah
a mitzvah you love to do?

אבגדהוזח**ט**יכלמנסעפצקרשת

טוּב הַבּוֹרֵא

The Goodness of the Creator

It's a mitzvah to love HASHEM
for all the wonderful things He gives us.
Look around and you'll see!

אבגדהוזח**ט**יכלמנסעפצקרשת

יָמִים טוֹבִים

ל

Jewish Festivals

Pesach, Shavuos, Succos —
HASHEM gave us these Yom Tov days
to be so extra happy!

אבגדהוזחטיכלמנסעפצקרשת

כְּבוֹד אָב וָאֵם כ
Honoring Father and Mother

Listening to your mother and father is such a big mitzvah.
So clean up your toys and make them proud of you.

א ב ג ד ה ו ז ח ט י **כ** ל מ נ ס ע פ צ ק ר ש ת

לוּלָב וְאֶתְרוֹג
Lulav and Esrog

Saying the brachah on the lulav and esrog on Succos,
then shaking them — that's a mitzvah too!

אבגדהוזחטיכ**ל**מנסעפצקרשת

מִשְׁלוֹחַ מָנוֹת
Mishloach Manos

Giving shalach manos on Purim is a mitzvah
that's so much fun. Please take a bite!

נֵרוֹת שַׁבָּת

Lighting Shabbos Candles

When candles are lit before Shabbos,
HASHEM makes your home happy and bright.

אבגדהוזחטיכלמנסעפצקרשת

סְפִירַת הָעוֹמֶר
Counting the Omer

ס

During Sefirah, don't forget to count the Omer
every single night!

אבגדהוזחטיכלמנס עפצקרשת

עֲבוֹדַת הַלֵּב (תְּפִילָה)
Prayer

ע

Davening is a special chance you get to ask HASHEM
for what is good and right.

אבגדהוזחטיכלמנסעפצקרשת

פֶּסַח

Passover

פ

On Pesach we eat matzah
and drink cups of wine — so many!

אבגדהוזחטיכלמנסע**פ**צקרשת

צְדָקָה
Charity

Your tzedakah helps poor people,
even when you drop in just a penny.

אבגדהוזחטיכלמנסעפצקרשת

קִדּוּשׁ

Kiddush

ק

Kiddush tells us that HASHEM made
the world in six days and rested on Shabbos,
and reminds us how the world was when it was new.

אבגדהוזחטיכלמנסעפצקרשת

רוֹדֵף שָׁלוֹם

Making Peace

What an important mitzvah it is to make peace,
to make people happy again —
you can do that too!

ר

אבגדהוזחטיכלמנסעפצקרשת

שְׁמִירַת כַּשְׁרוּת
Keeping Kosher

Eating Kosher foods is a mitzvah
that's so easy to do!

תּוֹרָה
Torah

But the greatest mitzvah of all is learning Torah.
It teaches you the mitzvos from א to ת,
all the way through!

אבגדהוזחטיכלמנסעפצקרשת

These mitzvos are given for you and for me.
Do them and you will feel so good — you'll see!

It will show everyone that you're a good Jew,
and HASHEM will be pleased and proud of you.